PAUL the PUCK

by PAULINA GALIARDI

kid at heart inc.

CALGARY FLAMES®

Kid at Heart Inc.
216 28th Avenue NE
Calgary, AB Canada T2E 5N1
www.kidatheart.ca

Ordering Information:
Quantity sales: Special discounts are available on quantity purchases
by corporations, associations, and others.
For details, contact the publisher at the address above.

Orders by Canadian trade bookstores and wholesalers:
Please contact LitDistCo : Phone: 1-800-591-6250
Fax: 1-800-591-6251 Email: orders@litdistco.ca
Address: 8300 Lawson Rd. Milton, ON, L9T 0A4

Printed in Canada.

This book is dedicated to the sport of hockey, the passion of its fans and the pucks that make it all possible.

There once was a puck and his name was Paul

He was an ordinary puck, nothing special at all.

But one thing he had
that set him apart

Was a career that he loved
and enjoyed with all his heart

He was a Flames puck
and played in the NHL

On the sticks of great players
who handled him well.

Paul knew the net
like the back of his hand
He got a thrill every time
he slipped past the goalie's pad

With a wrist shot, slap shot
or any other kind
Landing in the net
excited him out of his mind

The red light would glow,
the fans would all cheer
And Paul would be there,
smiling ear to ear.

He landed on the ice...

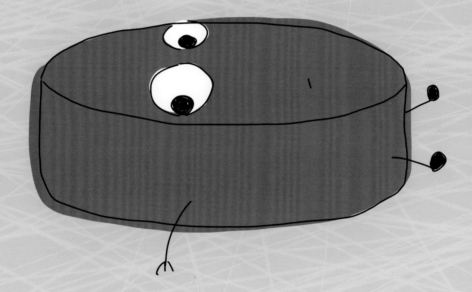

Did he make it, yes or no?

...Just another day for the Calgary Flames and Paul.

Paulina Galiardi has always felt inspired by the inherent wisdom, imagination and authenticity that children naturally possess, and this is why she felt called to write books for them. Paulina grew up in Toronto in a family of hockey-playing brothers and was surrounded by the culture and passion of the game from a very young age - which continued when she met her husband, former NHL forward TJ Galiardi.

In 2015, Paulina graduated from the prestigious Glenn Gould School of the Royal Conservatory of Music, where she trained to be a classical concert pianist. After years of performance and competition in the music world, Paulina decided that her heart was not fully in it, and longed to pursue something with more creative freedom and autonomy. She started writing children's poetry and drawing quirky cartoons in her spare time and eventually stumbled into the career that set her heart on fire - writing and illustrating children's books.

Paulina lives in Canada with her husband and their daughter Sage, as well as their two dogs.